Bucket List of a Chicken Sh*t

LONDON WEBB

LITERALLY LONDON WEBB, LLC

Contents

CHAPTER ONE

Meeting the Chicken

Yep, that's me, Sage Miller... sitting at my desk, soon to be replaced by the desk at home or the couch with my laptop, literally where the name indicates. It's what I do: work and work some more. Day in and day out, with little time or energy for anything beyond keeping the proverbial plates spinning. Vacations? Still working. Holidays? You guessed it, working. My entire life has become a series of To-Do lists I could never quite finish, punctuated by caffeine refills and apologetic text messages to the people I was constantly letting down.

Casinos are the only place I've found where my mind doesn't immediately latch onto work. Until the phone rings, that is. As soon as the call ends, I can usually stuff the stress back into its box and return to the flashing lights, the humming machines, and the sweet silence in my head. That silence feels like the first sip of a cold drink on a blistering day. For a little while, it's my happy place, a reprieve. But even then, it's temporary. Because when I leave, the noise always follows.

There has to be more, right? Some other way to quiet the chaos. Some other place or scenario where I could find peace without needing slot machines and synthetic carpet fumes to do the trick. The problem is, I'm a chicken shit. A big ball of nope, all tied up in a neat little bow of workaholism, two-day shipping, and Pinterest boards filled with things I'll probably never do.

In theory, I'd love to travel, pack a bag, and see something new. A place to feel the sun on my face without a meeting notification interrupting the moment. But the idea of disconnecting, really disconnecting, makes my chest tighten. I carry two phones everywhere—one for work, one personal—but in complete honesty, there's no distinction between them anymore. Both buzz with demands, both tether me to the grind. If I turned them off, I'd probably spend the first few hours twitching like an addict in withdrawal. The emails. The calls. The pings. The endless parade of "urgent" problems that apparently only I can solve.

Truth be told, I like being needed. Most days, anyway. There's a twisted sort of validation in it, like proof that I matter. But matter to who? The powers that be? The coworkers? The spreadsheets? What good is being indispensable to everyone else if I'm dispensable to myself?

They always say, "If you were to die tomorrow, your job would be posted before your obituary." And yet, that reality didn't sink in for me until the cracks started showing. The cracks became canyons the first night I woke up crying. I was dead asleep one second, and the next, I was sobbing like a toddler. The weight of everything found its way in at night and wouldn't let me ignore it.

That was when I knew what had to happen next. The workaholic chicken shit had to die. She had to pack up her excuses, her fears, her perfectly polished armor of competence and figure out how to live without constantly proving herself.

I started small. A bucket list because that's what you do, right? You write down all the things you've dreamed about but never thought you'd have the guts to do, and you tell yourself you're going to do them. Of course, writing a list and actually checking things off are two very different beasts. I'd written lists before. Hell, I'd made Excel spreadsheets of goals, color-coded them, and everything. But they always got buried under deadlines and emails. This time, though, it had to be different.

This time, it wasn't about impressing anyone or crossing something off just to say I did. This was about figuring out who I was when I wasn't glued to my desk or hiding behind my phones. Who was I when the noise stopped?

I didn't know the answer yet. But for the first time in years, I wanted to find out.

CHAPTER TWO

Chicken Soup

Those first few days of my resolve to pursue a phone-less, email-barren existence were tough. Like, punch-a-wall tough—not that I'd ever do that, but the thought crossed my mind more than once. I imagine it was akin to what most people felt during that short-lived TikTok shutdown. Except me, of course. Surprise... I don't do TikTok. Or Instagram. I tried once and, apparently, got booted for a reason I never bothered to investigate. My guess? Inactivity. Shocking, I know. Work always had 90 percent of my attention, a good book maybe 5 percent, and the remaining 5 percent was left to chance.

That's what I call the "chicken shit lottery." Spin the wheel and see if something worthwhile happens. Spoiler alert: it rarely does.

At first, it was hard to reprogram my brain to stop obsessing over all the things that wouldn't get done if I didn't do them. The emails piling up, the deadlines slipping further out of reach. It all used to feel so urgent. Then I reminded myself of something very important: I only get paid for 40 hours a week. Forty. Four-zero. And no matter how many extra hours I put in, how many fires I extinguished, or how many impossible tasks I magically pulled off, the outcome was always the same. The paychecks didn't get bigger, and the appreciation, IF it came, always felt hollow.

When I finally did the math, what I was actually making per hour, if you factored in the endless overtime, hit me like a ton of bricks. My fancy grown-up salary wasn't any better than the one I had fresh out of college, except now it came with three times the stress and half the excitement. Talk about not worth it.

So, I made a commitment to myself: no more extra hours. No more bending over backward to please people who wouldn't even remember my name if I left tomorrow. And I started my bucket list, finally.

Now, one thing about me is that I'm great at hyper-focusing. Give me a task, and I'll dive in so deep you'll have to send a search party to pull me out. Jotting down the first few items on my list? Piece of cake. Researching those items to death? Even easier. Google tabs open, YouTube tutorials playing in the background, and travel blogs bookmarked for "inspiration." I was a woman possessed. Several hours and only five items later, it hit me that I'd done it again. The very thing I was trying to escape, that endless cycle of overanalyzing, planning, and acting, had wormed its way into my bucket list. The very thing that was supposed to be about fun, spontaneity, and joy had turned into another freaking work project.

I'd burned that batch of chicken soup before I even got it on the stove.

And speaking of cooking—did I mention I'm terrible at it? Like, truly awful. It's one of the rare things I don't care about being good at. I own it. I cook when I absolutely have to, and even then, I'm counting down the seconds until I can shove the mess in the sink and order takeout. A cooking class? Not happening. Ever. If someone suggested adding it to my bucket list, I'd laugh in their face.

But then... I paused. What if that was it? What if the thing I hated the most, cooking, was actually the secret sauce I needed? Hear me out. If I could channel the same effort, energy, and borderline obsessive tendencies I normally poured into things I didn't love (like cooking) toward the things I actually wanted to do, maybe I could break this cycle. Perhaps I could stop turning everything into a chore and just, I don't know, do the damn thing. No spreadsheets, no flowcharts, no endless "research" to make sure I had all my ducks in a row. Just take action.

Maybe I needed to treat joy like a recipe. Find the ingredients, follow the steps, and let the thing simmer. Even if the first few attempts turn out burnt or bland, at least I'd be cooking something real, something for me. And who knows? Maybe I'd even get better at it. Not cooking. Let's not get carried away. But life? Yeah, maybe I could get better at that.

Chapter Three

Chicken Nuggets

One of the few things I cook well, and I only say that because it's truly dummy-proof, is chicken nuggets, the frozen kind, of course. Pop them in the oven, set the timer, and voila! Perfectly golden, crispy, and absolutely foolproof. Why can't my bucket list be more like that? Simple, straightforward, impossible to mess up. Easy enough to follow without overthinking, yet still satisfying. Nothing but a pure drive and desire to follow through on a plan that my brain, for once, wouldn't overcomplicate.

Here's the kicker: I'm even worse at spontaneity than I am at cooking. At least with cooking, I can follow a recipe. Spontaneity? That's just a freefall into chaos, and my brain doesn't do chaos. My brain is a professional "what if" machine, capable of imagining every possible worst-case scenario for every single idea, no matter how good it is. I could decide something was a brilliant idea, worthy of awards, even, and still manage to talk myself out of it within minutes. It's just how I operate. My default setting is paralysis by analysis.

If I'm being honest, Covid didn't do me any favors in that department. It took my already well-honed ability to avoid stepping out of my comfort zone and cranked it up to eleven. What if this? What if that? What if the world catches fire, and I'm in the middle of it? I mean, getting out and exploring was already hard enough before. The pandemic gave me a built-in excuse to just... stay home. At least in my head, it felt justified. But deep down? Deep down, I wanted something else. I wanted to explore. To see something different, to visit places that were strange and unique and worth remembering. I wanted to craft a list so epic it could win some mythical award for "Greatest Trip of All Time" (yes, I know that's not a real thing, but still). I wanted it for me, or at least for the version of me still buried under years of routines and excuses.

Venturing out with family was easier. Something about being "the adult" made public outings less overwhelming. I didn't have time to obsess over every little thing or second-guess myself because I was too busy making sure everyone else was okay. Count heads. Watch for cars. Don't let anyone eat gum off the sidewalk. You know, adulting. But when it came to stepping out on my own, for myself? That was a whole other story.

Could I do this? Could I make my bucket list as simple and foolproof as chicken nuggets? Could I pull off the perfectly golden, crispy exterior of adventure and find joy without the soggy mess of overthinking? Well, sure, in theory. Ideally. Maybe.

Oh crap.

Here it comes again, that spiral. The "what ifs." The doubts. The nagging voice in my head telling me I'll burn the nuggets, screw up the list, and wind up right back where I started: sitting at home, surrounded by half-finished plans and unopened possibilities. But then again, what if...

What if I didn't?

What if, for once, I ignored the voice, followed the plan, and trusted that the oven timer would ding at just the right moment? What if I didn't overthink it, didn't second-guess it, didn't give myself the chance to back out? What if I just did it?

One thing I know for sure: I'll never figure it out if I don't at least try.

CHAPTER FOUR

Frozen Chicken

Amazingly, the concept of thawing chicken put a lot into perspective for me. What had I been doing with my life? I'd packed myself away, sealed tight in some sodium-wash preservative, crammed into a bag with other frozen chicken shits, wasting away in the freezer. Waiting. For what, exactly? For someone else to decide I was worth thawing out? For some perfect moment to appear, as if life worked that way? The absurdity of it was almost laughable.

I started the list again for the second time.

Nothing fancy this time, no overthinking, no endless cycles of analysis and second-guessing. I grabbed a notebook and wrote down everything I wanted to do as if I were jotting down a grocery list. No worrying about how much it would cost or whether I'd need to learn a new language or deal with culture shock. Just pure, unfiltered desire. I want to go there. I want to do that. Simple. Everything else would work itself out.

In a way, I was thawing, too. The frozen chicken, with all its untapped potential, was starting to warm up to the idea of becoming something amazing. Perfectly seasoned and marinated in the zest of life. Suddenly, the world felt bigger and brighter, as if it had been waiting for me to wake up and notice it. Pictures in books or online were just shadows compared to the real thing, and I wanted to see the kind of beauty that could make me forget to breathe.

I decided to start small, close to home. Baby steps. I needed something to chip away at the frost, something to ease me out of my freezer bag existence and into the sunshine. I chose waterfalls. Tennessee had plenty to offer, and it was just the right mix of new and familiar. No passports, no planes, no overwhelming logistics—just me, a car, and some time to explore.

I left early on a Saturday, intentionally avoiding the temptation to make it more complicated than it needed to be. No vacation time, no itinerary, no stress. Just the open road and the promise of something different. It felt oddly liberating, almost rebellious, to shrug off the need for structure.

The first waterfall I stumbled upon was breathtaking. Standing there, with the roar of water crashing down from the rocks above, I felt the tension I'd been carrying for years start to dissolve. There was something humbling about being so close to that kind of power, something cleansing in the spray of the water. I hiked to several more waterfalls that day, each one a little different but all of them equally mesmerizing.

Somewhere along the way, I stopped at a rural dive bar for a drink. It was the kind of place with mismatched barstools and a jukebox that hadn't been updated since the early 2000s. I didn't plan to stay long, but somehow, I found myself striking up conversations with strangers, something I never would've done back home. For a fleeting moment, I even considered trying karaoke. I just considered it, mind you. The thought of standing up there, mic in hand, belting out a horribly off-key rendition of some cheesy pop song was almost enough to make me laugh out loud. Maybe one day. I might add it to the list, right next to cooking.

When I got back home Sunday afternoon, I felt different. Lighter, somehow. Clearer. Like I'd shaken off a layer of grime I hadn't even realized was there. The trip hadn't been extravagant or life-changing, but it didn't need to be. It was enough to make me believe there could be more trips like it, each one thawing me a little more, each one making me a little braver.

The chicken wasn't quite ready for the pan yet, but it was getting there. And for the first time in a long time, I was excited about the journey ahead.

CHAPTER FIVE

Thawing the Chicken

The second adventure wasn't something I planned weeks in advance or carefully mapped out. That was the point, after all—breaking free from my usual cycle of endless planning and just going. It had to be spontaneous, a gut decision that I'd follow through on without overanalyzing every possible outcome.

So, one Friday evening, as I scrolled through my phone (a habit I was working on), I came across a photo of hot air balloons floating serenely over a vast, open landscape. The colors were so vivid they looked like they'd been painted onto the sky. I stared at it for a while, something stirring inside me. I'd always been fascinated by hot air balloons, their quiet majesty, and the idea of drifting weightlessly above it all. It was romantic, in a way, and so far removed from the chaos of everyday life.

I googled "hot air balloon rides near me." A small town about two hours away was hosting a balloon festival that weekend, complete with rides, food trucks, and live music. Without giving myself time to think, I booked a spot on one of the flights for Saturday evening. Just like that, I had my next adventure.

The drive there was uneventful, but as I pulled into the festival grounds, I could feel a mixture of excitement and nerves bubbling up. The field was alive with activity. Kids chase each other with sticky cotton candy fingers. Couples hold hands as they wander past stalls selling crafts and trinkets, and, of course, the balloons. Dozens of them, their vibrant colors and patterns standing out against the blue sky.

When it was my turn to board the basket, I hesitated for just a second. What if I hated it? What if I panicked the moment we left the ground? But I took a deep breath, told my inner chicken shit to shut up, and climbed in.

The moment the balloon lifted, all those worries melted away. The ground fell away in a slow, gentle motion, and the world unfolded beneath me. Fields, rivers, and rooftops, all stretched out in perfect harmony, bathed in the soft glow of the setting sun. The silence was breathtaking. It wasn't the heavy, suffocating silence I felt when I was stressed or burnt out. This was a peaceful kind of quiet, one that made me feel small in the best possible way.

The pilot pointed out landmarks as we floated, but I barely registered what he was saying. I was too busy soaking it all in, committing every detail to memory. The cool breeze against my skin. The faint smell of propane from the burner. The way the colors of the landscape seemed to shift as the sun dipped lower. For the first time in ages, I felt completely present, completely alive.

After the ride, the passengers all gathered for a champagne toast. I sipped mine slowly, letting the warmth of the moment sink in. I didn't know these people, but for that brief stretch of time, we were connected by the shared experience of floating above the world.

On the drive home, I couldn't stop smiling. The kind of smile that comes from somewhere deep inside, the kind you can't fake. It wasn't just the balloon ride that left me feeling lighter. It was knowing I'd done it. I'd stepped out of my comfort zone, silenced the doubts, and allowed myself to experience something new.

The chicken ready to thaw, no doubt about it. One adventure at a time, I was learning how to live outside the freezer. And as I thought about what might come next, I realized something important: I wasn't afraid anymore. Excited, yes. Nervous, maybe. But fear? That was back in the bag with the other chicken shits.

CHAPTER SIX

Chicken Seasoning

One of those rare moments when I wasn't glued to a screen presented me with my next adventure. I was walking past the park near my house, enjoying the quiet of a late afternoon, when I noticed a group of people gathered near a trailhead. They were dressed in hiking gear, backpacks, and sturdy boots. One of them was holding a map. The thought came out of nowhere: What if I went hiking?

It wasn't exactly groundbreaking. People went hiking all the time. But for me, the idea of wandering off into the woods with nothing but a trail to follow was a little unnerving. What if I got lost? What if it rained? What if

I slipped and broke my ankle and had to be airlifted out like one of those cautionary tales on the news?

But then another thought pushed its way in: What if it's exactly what I need?

That Saturday, I woke up early, pulled on some sneakers I was pretty sure were not meant for hiking, and headed to the nearest state park. The drive was short, less than an hour, and as I pulled into the parking lot, I felt a familiar mix of excitement and nerves. There was no turning back now. I grabbed a small backpack I'd hastily packed with a water bottle, a granola bar, and one phone (just in case) and headed toward the trailhead.

The air smelled like pine and damp earth, and the sound of birds filled the quiet. The trail was marked as "moderate," which seemed like a safe choice for a first-timer. As I started walking, I kept my pace slow, letting myself take in the scenery. Trees arched overhead, their leaves filtering the sunlight into dappled patterns on the ground. A small creek ran alongside the trail, its water clear and cool.

At first, I couldn't turn off my brain. I kept checking the map I'd grabbed at the ranger station, mentally calculating how long it would take to complete the loop and whether I'd packed enough snacks. But eventually, as the trail curved deeper into the woods, something shifted. The usual stream of anxious thoughts slowed, then stopped altogether. It was just me and the rhythm of my footsteps, the sound of the creek, and the occasional rustle of leaves as a squirrel darted past.

About halfway through, the trail opened up to a small overlook. I stood there for a while, looking out at the valley below, the green expanse stretching all the way to the horizon. The world felt vast and still, and for the first time in a long time, I wasn't thinking about work, emails, or deadlines. I was just... there. Present.

When I reached the end of the trail, I felt an odd mix of exhaustion and exhilaration. My legs ached in a way that reminded me I'd actually used them for something other than sitting at a desk. My sneakers were caked in mud, my face was flushed, and I probably smelled like a mix of sweat and bug spray, but I didn't care. I felt alive.

On the way home, I stopped at a small roadside stand selling fresh fruit and homemade pies. I bought a slice of peach pie and sat on the tailgate of my car to eat it, the sticky sweetness of the peaches balancing perfectly with the flaky crust. It felt like a little reward for stepping out of my comfort zone.

That hike wasn't just a walk in the woods. It was a reminder that I could handle more than I gave myself credit for. I could step into the unknown and not only survive but enjoy it. The chicken was almost ready for the pan, and I could feel the momentum building.

CHAPTER SEVEN

Into the Pan

Whitewater rafting was one of those things I'd always admired from afar. It seemed so wild, so exhilarating, so... not me. But after the hike, I was itching for something that would push me even further outside my comfort zone. I didn't just want to explore. I wanted to feel alive.

When I saw a flyer at the state park visitor center advertising whitewater rafting trips on a nearby river, I snapped a picture of it without thinking twice. That same night, I booked a half-day beginner's trip. The words beginner-friendly in bold letters gave me just enough courage to hit the confirm button.

The morning of the trip, I felt the nerves creeping in as I drove toward the river. What if I fell out of the raft? What if I couldn't paddle fast enough? What if I hated it and spent the whole time wishing I were back on solid ground? But I'd made a promise to myself... no more talking myself out of adventures. No more letting fear win.

I arrived at the outfitter's base camp, and the energy was contagious. People were milling around in bright helmets and life jackets, chatting excitedly as guides called out instructions. After a quick safety briefing that included how to survive if I did fall out (not comforting, by the way), we were split into groups and loaded into rafts. My guide, a sunburned guy named Travis, assured us that as long as we listened to his commands, we'd be fine.

"Trust the river," he said with a quick grin. I wasn't sure I trusted the river, or Travis, for that matter, but I nodded along anyway.

The first stretch of the river was calm, almost deceivingly so. The raft drifted lazily, and I started to relax, even dipping my hand into the cold, clear water.

But then I heard it, the distant roar of rapids ahead. My grip on the paddle tightened, and my stomach did a little flip as we approached the first set of whitewater.

"Forward paddle!" Travis yelled, and we dug in, paddling hard as the raft surged forward. Water splashed over the sides, drenching us in seconds, and my heart pounded as we hit the first drop. For a moment, I couldn't tell if I was screaming or laughing, or both.

The rapids came in waves, each one a little more thrilling than the last. There was something primal about it, the way the river seemed alive, unpredictable, and powerful. I stopped worrying about falling out or messing up and just let myself feel it. The rush of the water, the spray against my face, the burn in my arms as I paddled. It was terrifying and exhilarating all at once.

There were calmer stretches in between, moments where we floated quietly while the scenery unfolded around us. Towering cliffs, emerald green trees, and the occasional bald eagle soaring overhead. Those moments felt just as powerful as the rapids, a reminder that nature could be both fierce and gentle.

By the time we reached the end of the trip, I was soaked to the bone; my muscles were aching, and I couldn't stop smiling. The group all high-fived as we pulled the raft onto the shore, laughing at our near misses and reliving the biggest drops. Travis grinned at me and said, "Told you the river would take care of you."

On the drive home, I replayed the day in my head, still riding the adrenaline high: the fear, the excitement, the pure, unfiltered joy. I'd felt it all, and I'd come out the other side stronger for it.

This adventure wasn't just about the rapids. It was about learning to trust myself, to lean into the unknown to see where it could take me. The chicken was definitely thawed now, meeting the pan with that unmistakable sound as it begins to find the perfect temperature.

As I pulled into my driveway, exhausted but happy, I couldn't help but wonder: What could top this?

CHAPTER EIGHT

Searing the Chicken

Ziplining was an adventure had been brewing for a while, and it scared me, but in a way, that excited me just enough to say yes. Something about soaring through the treetops, suspended by a thin cable, felt equal parts exhilarating and terrifying. It wasn't the heights that got to me. I wasn't exactly a fan, but I could deal with them. It was "the trust". Trusting the equipment, trusting the guides, and mostly, trusting myself to just let go.

I found a place about three hours away that offered a ziplining course through a dense canopy of old-growth forest. The description promised breathtaking views, suspension bridges, and the "ultimate adrenaline rush." I booked it without hesitation, knowing that if I stopped to think about it too long, I'd talk myself out of it. The old me would've done just that, but I wasn't who I once was. Or at least, I was trying not to be.

When I arrived, the guides were cheerful and upbeat, which helped ease the nerves bubbling up as they strapped me into the harness. They went over the safety procedures, cracking jokes to lighten the mood, but all I could focus on was the platform looming in the distance, the one where I'd be taking my first leap.

The first zip was a short one meant to ease us into it. Baby steps, right? When it was my turn, I shuffled to the edge of the platform, gripping the harness like my life depended on it. The guide smiled at me and said, "Just lean into it. The hardest part is the first step."

I nodded, not trusting myself to speak, and before I could chicken out, I stepped off the edge.

The initial drop was a blur of adrenaline and wind, but then something shifted. The rush of fear melted into something else entirely. Freedom. Pure, unadulterated freedom. The cable hummed above me as I zipped through the air, the forest rushing past in a blur of green. The trees stretched out below like an endless sea, and for those few seconds, it felt like flying.

By the time I reached the second platform, I was grinning so hard my cheeks hurt. The guides were already cheering me on, and I felt something I hadn't felt in a long time: pride. It wasn't the kind of pride that came from checking off a task at work or meeting a deadline, but the kind that came from doing something just for myself.

The rest of the course was a mix of zips, suspension bridges, and even a rappel down to the forest floor. Each zipline seemed higher and faster than the last, and with each step off the platform, I felt alive. The fear was still there, a low hum in the background, but it was no longer in control.

By the time we finished, I was buzzing with energy. My legs were a little shaky, and my arms ached from gripping the harness, but none of that mattered. What mattered was that I'd done it. I'd stepped off the edge, again and again, and let myself soar.

Driving home that evening, I thought about what the guide had said: "The hardest part is the first step." Wasn't that the truth? Every adventure I'd taken so far had started with one small, scary step. But each step had led to something bigger, something better. The chicken wasn't just thawed now—it was sizzling, searing with the kind of heat that made it impossible to go back to the freezer.

As I pulled into my driveway, the sky painted in shades of pink and gold, I couldn't help but feel a little invincible. The old me would've been proud of how far I'd come. The new me? She was already looking ahead, ready for the next leap.

CHAPTER NINE

Turning Brown

A spur-of-the-moment Google search led to my next adventure: unique experiences near me. It wasn't exactly inspired, but I figured something interesting would pop up, and it did. About an hour away, there was an outdoor rock-climbing gym built into the side of an old quarry. The pictures looked surreal. Massive stone walls rising up from the earth, dotted with colorful climbing holds. Climbers dangled from ropes like tiny, determined ants scaling a cliff. It was intimidating just to look at, but that's why I clicked the "book now" button.

I'd never climbed anything before. Not a wall, not a tree, well, unless you count the time I tried to scramble up a cherry tree as a kid and ended up with a scraped knee and a bruised ego. But something about this felt different. It wasn't just about the physical challenge; it was about finding a new kind of strength, both in my body and in myself.

When I arrived, the staff at the quarry gym were welcoming and encouraging. They fitted me with a harness and gave me a quick rundown of the basics: how to belay, how to find good handholds, and, most importantly, how to fall safely if I needed to. That last part didn't do much to calm my nerves, but I nodded along like I had a clue what I was doing.

The first wall I attempted was one of the easier routes, or so they said. As I stared up at it, craning my neck to see the top, I wasn't so sure. My palms were already sweaty, and I hadn't even started. The instructor clipped me into the rope, smiled reassuringly, and said, "Take your time. One step at a time. Trust your feet."

With a deep breath, I reached for the first hold. My muscles protested almost immediately, unused to the strain, but I kept going. Hand over hand, foot over foot, I inched my way up the wall. It wasn't graceful—I slipped more than once and clung to the holds like a koala gripping a branch—but I didn't stop.

About halfway up, I paused to catch my breath and looked out at the quarry. The view was incredible. The sun was high in the sky, casting golden light over the stone walls and the surrounding forest. I hadn't even reached the top yet, but I already felt a rush of accomplishment.

When I finally made it to the top, I let out a laugh, part relief, part triumph. The instructor below cheered, and I grinned down at him as he called up, "Ready to rappel?" My heart jumped a little, but I nodded. The idea of leaning back and trusting the rope to hold me felt unnatural, but after a few shaky steps, I got the hang of it. The descent was almost as exhilarating as the climb, and by the time my feet hit the ground, I was buzzing with adrenaline.

I tackled a few more routes that day, each one a little harder than the last. There were moments where I doubted myself, where my grip slipped, and my arms screamed for a break, but I kept pushing. And with each climb, I learned to trust myself a little more.

By the end of the day, my hands were raw, my arms felt like jelly, and my legs ached from the effort, but I couldn't stop smiling. I'd done something I never thought I could do, something that had seemed impossible just a few hours earlier.

I replayed the day in my mind, the feeling of standing at the top of the wall and looking out over the quarry. There was something transformative about climbing, about struggling upward, one move at a time, and reaching a place you didn't think you could. It felt like a metaphor for everything I'd been trying to do with my life.

The chicken was no longer just sizzling. It was starting to crisp, golden, and delicious, ready for what lies ahead.

CHAPTER TEN

Flipping the Chicken

T he next excursion found me, as adventures
sometimes do, disguised as an innocent coffee
stop at a roadside café. I was heading back from a long
weekend exploring a small town known for its quirky
antique shops and hiking trails. My legs were tired, my
mind was full of new memories, and I needed caffeine for
the drive home.

The café was the kind of place that could've been
plucked straight out of a movie. A cozy little cabin with
a wraparound porch, mismatched furniture, and a menu
scrawled in colorful chalk above the counter. I ordered
a latte and a muffin, found a seat near the window, and

pulled out my bucket list notebook to jot down a few thoughts.

That's when I saw him.

He walked in with a camera slung over his shoulder, wearing a slightly rumpled button-down and jeans. He had that casual, I'm-not-trying-too-hard kind of confidence that immediately caught my attention. But it wasn't just the way he looked; it was the way he moved as if he was curious about the world and completely at ease in it. He ordered coffee, scanned the room, and his eyes landed on me.

"Mind if I join you?" he asked, gesturing to the empty chair across from me.

Normally, I'd have stammered out some excuse, but something about him felt... easy. Like saying no would've been harder than saying yes. I nodded, and just like that, a conversation began.

His name was Sam, and he was a freelance photographer traveling through the area for a project. We talked about his work, the places he'd been, and the places he wanted to go. When he asked what I was doing, I hesitated. Telling someone about my bucket list felt vulnerable, almost like admitting I didn't have it all figured out. But I told him anyway.

Instead of laughing or brushing it off, he leaned forward, genuinely interested. "So, what's next on the list?" he asked.

"Horseback riding," I blurted out, surprising even myself. I hadn't written it down yet, but it had been lingering in the back of my mind for weeks.

"Funny," he said with a grin. "I know a place just a few miles from here. They do trail rides. Want to check it out?"

I hesitated. Riding a horse had always seemed like one of those things other people did—people with confidence and balance and some inherent understanding of animals I didn't have. But there he was, looking at me with a mix of excitement and encouragement, and before I knew it, I was saying yes.

The trail ride was a mix of terror and magic. Sam, of course, looked perfectly at home in the saddle, chatting easily with the guide as his horse plodded along. I, on the other hand, spent the first twenty minutes clinging to the reins for dear life as if they alone would anchor me when my butt decided the ground was more suitable than the saddle. But as the ride went on, I started to relax. The rhythmic sway of the horse, the soft crunch of hooves on the trail, and the way the sunlight filtered through the trees were enough to make me forget my nerves.

At one point, we stopped at a clearing with a view of the valley below. It was breathtaking, the kind of scene that didn't feel real until you were standing in it. Sam pulled out his camera and started snapping photos, occasionally glancing over at me with a smile.

"Stay there," he said, pointing to the edge of the clearing. "The light's perfect."

I laughed nervously but stayed put as he clicked away. It felt strange, being the subject of someone else's focus, but there was something about the way he looked at me, like he wasn't just taking a picture but capturing a moment.

By the time we made it back to the stables, the sun was dipping low on the horizon. We lingered a little longer, talking and laughing until it was clear neither of us wanted the day to end.

Over the next few weeks, Sam and I kept in touch. We met up a few more times. Another trail ride, a spontaneous road trip to a nearby art festival, and a quiet night watching the stars from the back of his truck. There was something easy and fleeting about it like we both knew it wouldn't last but didn't care. He had his life on the road, and I had mine, but for a little while, our paths overlapped in the most unexpected, beautiful way.

When he left for his next project, we parted on good terms, with no promises or dramatic goodbyes. It wasn't sad, not really. It was exactly what it needed to be: a short chapter that added color to my story without taking it over.

As I watched his truck disappear down the road, I felt something I hadn't expected: gratitude. For the adventure, for the connection, and for the reminder that not everything in life has to be permanent to matter.

Sam had given me something I hadn't even realized I was missing. A push to take chances, to embrace the unknown, and to trust that sometimes, the best moments come when you stop trying to control them.

The chicken wasn't perfect just yet, but every day it sizzled a little more.

CHAPTER ELEVEN

Sea Chicken

I was starting to realize that an unexpected adventure was the best kind, and this one began with a flyer tacked to the bulletin board of a coffee shop. "Sailing Lessons – No Experience Needed." The picture of a sailboat gliding across calm water, its sails billowing in the wind, caught my eye immediately. Sailing had always seemed like one of those things reserved for people who wore boat shoes and owned yachts, but the idea of being out on the open water, with nothing but the wind to guide me, was tempting.

I took a picture of the flyer, and by the time I left the coffee shop, I'd signed up for a weekend beginner's course at a marina two hours away.

When I arrived, I was greeted by a mix of excitement and nerves. The marina was bustling with activity. Boats rocking gently in their slips, seagulls squawking overhead, and people moving purposefully along the docks. Our group of beginners gathered near a small sailboat, and that's when I noticed him.

His name was Lucas, and he was one of the instructors. He looked like he belonged on a boat. Tanned skin, wind-tousled hair, and the kind of relaxed confidence that comes from spending years on the water. He introduced himself to the group with an easy smile, explaining the basics of sailing in a way that made it sound less daunting than I'd imagined.

"Don't overthink it," he said as we climbed aboard. "The boat knows what to do. You just have to listen to it."

That was easier said than done. The first time I tried to steer, I nearly sent us careening into another boat. Lucas caught the tiller just in time, his hand brushing mine as he steadied it.

"Relax," he said, his voice calm and steady. "You're overcorrecting. Feel the movement, don't fight it."

I nodded, trying to focus on his words instead of the way his hand lingered on mine for just a second too long.

As the day went on, I started to find my rhythm. The wind filled the sails, the water rushed past the hull, and for the first time, I felt like I was a part of something bigger. Sailing wasn't just about controlling the boat; it was about working with the elements and adapting to the wind and the waves.

By the end of the first day, I was hooked. After the lesson, a few of us stayed behind to help secure the boat and swap stories about our first attempts. Lucas hung back, too, leaning casually against the railing as he listened.

"Not bad for your first day," he said when the others wandered off.

"Not bad? I almost took out another boat," I laughed.

"Yeah, but you didn't. That's what matters."

There was a pause, the kind of silence that felt full rather than awkward. Then he said, "A few of us are grabbing dinner at the harbor later. You should come."

It wasn't a date, at least not officially, but something about the way he said it made my heart skip a beat. I said yes.

Dinner was lively, with the group sharing laughs and swapping stories over fresh seafood and cold drinks. Lucas sat next to me, and we fell into an easy conversation, talking about everything from his years on the water to my bucket list adventures. He had a way of making me feel at ease like I could tell him anything, and he'd actually care.

Throughout the weekend, there were more moments like that. A shared laugh as I struggled to tie a proper knot. His steady encouragement as I took the helm again, this time with a little more confidence. The way his eyes lit up when he talked about his dream of sailing across the world someday.

There was an undeniable connection, but it wasn't rushed or overwhelming. It was like the wind on the water: present, steady, and natural. By the end of the weekend, I'd learned the basics of sailing and found something even more surprising: the possibility of something deeper with someone who seemed to understand the pull of adventure as much as I did.

When it was time to leave, Lucas walked me to my car.

"You've got a good instinct for this," he said, his hands in his pockets. "And if you ever want to get back out on the water, you know where to find me."

"Careful," I teased. "I might take you up on that."

"I'm counting on it."

The drive home was bittersweet, a mix of excitement about what I'd accomplished and the lingering anticipation of what might lie ahead. Lucas wasn't Sam. This wasn't a whirlwind romance or a fleeting connection. It felt slower, like the beginning of something with potential. But I wasn't rushing it. If there was one thing I'd learned from sailing, it was to let the wind take you where it will.

The chicken was almost golden now, its flavor deepening with every new experience. And as I thought about Lucas and the open water, I couldn't help but smile. The wind was blowing in just the right direction.

CHAPTER TWELVE

Chicken Half-Cooked

The next adventure was more personal and quieter. It wasn't about checking off another bold item on my bucket list or diving headfirst into the unknown. It was about saying yes to Lucas's invitation, about trusting the pull I felt toward him and letting myself see where it might lead.

A few weeks after the sailing weekend, Lucas texted me: "How do you feel about a sunset sail? Just us this time. Bring snacks."

It was simple and low-pressure, but the thought of spending an evening on the water with him made my stomach flutter. I packed a small bag with a bottle of wine, some cheese, crackers, and a couple of chocolate bars for good measure and met him at the marina on a warm Friday evening.

Lucas was already there, adjusting the lines on a small sailboat. The light was soft and golden, and it cast him in a way that made me pause for a second before calling out, "I hope you're ready for a snack feast."

He looked up, grinning. "Always."

As we pushed off from the dock, the water was calm, the kind of serene that made it feel like the world was holding its breath. Lucas worked the sails with an easy confidence I'd come to admire, and I sat on the bench, watching him.

"You've done this a million times, haven't you?" I said.

"Pretty much," he admitted. "But it never gets old. There's always something different out here. A new wind, a different light... It's never the same twice."

I could see what he meant. As the boat glided across the water, the colors of the sunset shifted, painting the horizon in shades of orange, pink, and violet. The air was warm, the kind of summer evening that wraps around you like a soft blanket, and the only sound was the gentle lapping of the waves against the hull.

We dropped anchor near a quiet cove, and Lucas joined me with a blanket he'd stashed in the cabin. I pulled out the wine and snacks, and we sat side by side, sharing stories as we ate. I told him about my bucket list, the hikes and waterfalls, the whitewater rafting, and even my frozen-chicken metaphor. He laughed at that, his eyes crinkling in a way that made me laugh, too.

"I like the way you think," he said after a while. "You've got this way of finding meaning in everything."

I shrugged, suddenly self-conscious. "It's just how my brain works, I guess. Overthinking everything until I can turn it into a metaphor."

"It's not overthinking," he said, his voice quieter now. "It's paying attention. Most people don't."

The way he said it made my chest ache in a way I couldn't quite explain. It wasn't what he said. It was the way he said it. He saw something in me that I wasn't even sure I saw myself.

As the stars started to appear, he leaned back against the bench and pointed out constellations, naming them like old friends. I listened, asking questions and letting myself be fully in the moment. There was no room for overthinking here, no space for my usual "what ifs." Just the two of us, the boat rocking gently beneath us, and the vast, open sky above.

At some point, the conversation slowed, and we sat in comfortable silence. I leaned against him, his arm draped lightly around my shoulders, and for the first time in what felt like forever, I felt truly at peace.

"You know," he said after a while, his voice soft, "you're kind of amazing."

I laughed, shaking my head. "You barely know me."

"Maybe," he said, tilting his head to look at me. "But I'd like to change that."

The words hung in the air, weightless and full of possibility. I looked at him, his face lit faintly by the moonlight, and something in me shifted. It wasn't dramatic or overwhelming; it was steady like a tide rising slowly but surely.

"I'd like that too," I said, my voice barely above a whisper.

We stayed out on the water until the moon was high in the sky, talking and laughing and falling into something that felt deeper than just an adventure. It wasn't rushed, wasn't forced. It was like the wind on the sails, natural and unhurried, guiding us in the direction we were meant to go.

The chicken wasn't just sizzling now—it was transforming, infused with a flavor I hadn't expected. As Lucas steered us back toward the marina, his hand brushing against mine, I realized that this adventure wasn't just about the bucket list.

Maybe it was about finding the kind of connection I hadn't even known I was searching for.

CHAPTER THIRTEEN

Chicken Pairing

For the first time in this bucket list journey, I had the company of Lucas. After the sailing lessons, we'd kept in touch, texting back and forth about everything from travel ideas to silly memes. It started casually but grew into something more. When he suggested a weekend kayaking trip to a secluded chain of islands off the coast, I couldn't say no.

Kayaking wasn't something I'd ever considered for the list, but the idea of gliding across the water and exploring untouched beaches and hidden coves sounded perfect. Plus, the thought of spending more time with Lucas was... well, let's just say I was excited in a way I hadn't been in a long time.

We met at the marina early Saturday morning, the sun barely cresting over the horizon. Lucas was already there, unloading the kayaks, his easy grin setting me instantly at ease. He walked me through the basics: how to paddle efficiently, what to do if I tipped over (a terrifying yet slightly thrilling prospect), and how to pack the kayak so it wouldn't sink.

"Don't worry," he said, handing me a life jacket. "I'll make sure you don't drift off into the Atlantic."

We set out, the world around us quiet except for the rhythmic splash of our paddles cutting through the water. The islands came into view slowly, their rocky shorelines dotted with lush greenery. It felt like we were stepping into a postcard, the kind of place you can't quite believe exists until you see it for yourself.

As we paddled closer, Lucas's kayak drifted alongside mine. "You're a natural," he said, the teasing edge in his voice making me roll my eyes.

"Yeah, I'm sure that's what you said to all your students," I shot back, grinning.

"Only the ones who don't paddle in circles," he said with a wink.

We spent the day exploring the islands, finding hidden trails, wading through tide pools, and even daring a chilly swim in the crystal-clear water. It was easy and comfortable. The connection between us deepened with every laugh and every shared moment, and I found myself wondering if this could be more than just another short-lived romance.

Just as everything felt like it was falling into place, reality decided to make an unwelcome appearance.

We were sitting by the campfire that night, sharing a bottle of wine and talking about our favorite childhood memories, when Lucas's phone buzzed. He glanced at the screen, and the relaxed smile on his face disappeared, replaced by something harder to read.

"Everything okay?" I asked, trying to keep my tone light.

He hesitated, then sighed. "It's Emily. My ex."

I didn't know much about Emily. They'd dated for a while and broken up months before I met him. But the look on his face told me she wasn't quite out of the picture.

"She's... going through some stuff," he said finally, setting the phone down beside him. "We've stayed in touch, and I guess she's struggling right now."

I nodded, trying to keep my expression neutral, but my stomach was doing somersaults. "Do you need to call her back?"

"No," he said quickly, too quickly. "Not right now. This is our weekend."

I wanted to believe him, but a small part of me couldn't shake the feeling that Emily was more than just a distant ex. The way his mood shifted so abruptly, the way he looked at his phone like it was a tether to something vital. It all gnawed at me, even as I tried to push it aside.

The next day, as we paddled back to the mainland, the easy rhythm we'd fallen into felt a little off. Lucas was quieter and more distracted, and though he smiled and laughed when I joked, there was something distant in his eyes.

I didn't bring it up. Not then. I told myself it wasn't the right time, and I didn't want to ruin the adventure. But deep down, I knew we'd have to talk about it eventually. Because as much as I wanted to trust what we were building, the shadow of his past was starting to cast a long shadow over the present.

The chicken wasn't quite burning, but it was dangerously close to sticking to the pan. As I drove home later that day, my heart felt heavier than it should've after such an incredible weekend.

This was new territory for me. Bucket list adventures were one thing, but navigating the uncharted waters of a relationship, complete with unexpected storms? That was something else entirely. But if I'd learned anything on this journey, it was that sometimes, you just have to paddle through the rough patches and hope the water smooths out on the other side.

I wasn't sure where Lucas and I were heading, but one thing was certain: this wasn't the end of the adventure. Not yet.

CHAPTER FOURTEEN

Side Dishes

My connection with Lucas felt both exhilarating and unsettling, like standing on the edge of a cliff with the wind whipping around me. Every moment we spent together intensified those feelings, whether it was kayaking, grabbing dinner at a hole-in-the-wall seafood shack, or sitting on the dock after hours, watching the moonlight dance across the water. I felt seen and heard, and I was able to let my guard down in a way I hadn't in years. But just beneath the surface, something else lingered. The shadow of Emily was always there, a quiet but persistent reminder that I wasn't the only one vying for his attention.

It started small. A text here, a phone call there, moments when his phone buzzed, and his expression changed. He always brushed it off, but each interaction left a crack in the easy rhythm we'd built. And I hated how much it bothered me. It wasn't like I didn't trust him, but the situation felt murky, undefined, and messy.

One evening, we were sitting on the deck of Lucas's sailboat, watching the sun dip below the horizon. He had his arm draped over my shoulders, and for a moment, everything felt perfect. Then his phone buzzed again. He didn't reach for it, didn't even glance at it, but the tension in his body was unmistakable.

"You can answer it," I said, trying to sound casual, even though my chest felt tight.

He sighed, running a hand through his hair. "It's just Emily. I'll call her back later."

"She calls a lot," I said, not accusing, just observing.

"She's still having a rough time," he said, his voice softer now, almost apologetic. "I don't want to abandon her, you know? But..." He hesitated, looking at me. "I don't want it to interfere with us either."

"Is it interfering?" I asked, the question slipping out before I could stop it.

He didn't answer right away, and that silence said more than words ever could.

That night, I drove home with my thoughts spiraling. Part of me wanted to trust him completely, to believe him when he said I was the one he wanted to be with. But another part of me, the part that had spent years second-guessing myself and playing it safe, couldn't shake the doubt. I didn't want to be a placeholder or someone's escape while they figured out what they really wanted.

The old me would've let this doubt fester, stewing silently until I convinced myself to back away altogether. Not now though. The chicken shit was gone, replaced by someone who wasn't afraid to stand up for herself, even when it was uncomfortable.

The next time I saw Lucas, I didn't wait for the perfect moment. As we sat by the water, the sun sparkling on the waves, I turned to him and said, "Lucas, I need to talk to you about Emily."

He looked surprised but nodded. "Okay. What's on your mind?"

"I need to know where we stand," I said, my voice steady even though my heart was racing. "I like you, Lucas, a lot. But I can't keep doing this if there's still something unresolved with her. I'm not asking you to cut her out of your life, but I need to know that I'm not just a distraction or someone to fill the space while you figure things out."

He stared at me for a moment, his brow furrowed, weighing his words carefully. "You're not a distraction," he said finally. "And you're not filling a space. I care about you more than I thought I would. But... Emily's been a part of my life for a long time. We're not together, and we never will be again, but I feel responsible for her. I don't want to hurt her."

I nodded, taking in his words. "I get that, but you need to realize that by trying to protect her, you're hurting us. I'm not asking you to stop being there for her, but I need to know that I'm your priority. That this", I gestured between us, "is what you want."

He reached for my hand, his grip warm and steady. "This is what I want," he said, his voice firm. "You're what I want. I'll talk to Emily and set some boundaries. I owe her that, but I owe you that too."

The relief I felt was tempered by the knowledge that this wasn't the end of the conflict. Relationships, I realized, weren't about neatly tied-up resolutions. They were about navigating the messiness together, about being willing to have hard conversations and face uncomfortable truths.

Driving home that night, I felt a quiet sense of pride. Not because everything had been magically resolved but because I hadn't backed down. I'd spoken my truth, set my boundaries, and made it clear what I needed. The old me would've avoided the confrontation altogether, retreating into my shell of fear and overthinking.

The chicken was no longer just thawed or sizzling, and it hadn't stuck to the pan. It was strong, flavorful, and holding its own. And so was I. Whatever the future holds, I knew I could handle it. I wasn't afraid to take up space, to ask for what I deserved, and trust in my strength.

CHAPTER FIFTEEN

Turning Down the Heat

The connection with Lucas was growing stronger, but so was the weight of everything that came with him. It wasn't just the time we spent together sailing, kayaking, exploring tiny beach towns, or just sitting in comfortable silence on the dock by his boat. It was the way he listened, the way he looked at me like I was someone worth believing in, even when I doubted myself.

No matter how easy things felt between us in those moments, the shadow of his ex-girlfriend, Emily, seemed to follow us everywhere. At first, it was just the occasional text or call, moments I could overlook because Lucas always reassured me that it was nothing. But "nothing" started to feel like "something" when her texts became more frequent, her calls more insistent, and her presence more invasive.

The escalation felt like it came out of nowhere, or maybe I just hadn't been paying close enough attention. It happened one evening when Lucas and I were supposed to meet for dinner at a little seafood place by the harbor. I was waiting at the table, sipping a glass of wine and watching the sunset, when Lucas walked in, his expression tight and his shoulders tense.

"Sorry I'm late," he said, dropping into the chair across from me.

"What happened?" I asked, already knowing the answer.

"Emily showed up at the marina," he said, rubbing the back of his neck. "She was upset. Something about feeling abandoned, because I've been ignoring her."

I set my glass down, the warm buzz of excitement I'd felt earlier now replaced with a sinking feeling in my stomach. "And what did you say?"

"I told her I care about her as a friend, but I'm not responsible for her happiness. I told her about us."

That caught me off guard. "You told her about us?"

He nodded, his eyes meeting mine. "She needed to hear it. She needs to know that I've moved on."

"And how did she take it?"

He hesitated, and that told me everything I needed to know.

"She didn't take it well," he admitted. "But I think it's for the best. She has to let go."

I wanted to believe him, to trust that this was the turning point, but something in my gut told me this wasn't over. And I was right.

A few days later, Emily messaged me. I don't even know how she got my number, but there it was, a long, rambling text about how Lucas was leading her on, how they had too much history to just let it go, and how I was some sort of obstacle in their "unfinished story." I stared at the screen, my heart pounding, a mix of anger and doubt rising in my chest.

The old me would've ignored it. I would've buried the feelings, avoided confrontation, and quietly let the situation eat away at me until I convinced myself to walk away, but I was no longer the old me.

I texted Lucas immediately, asking him to meet me at the marina.

When I arrived, he was already there, sitting on the edge of the dock with his feet dangling over the water. He looked up as I approached, his face softening when he saw me.

"She texted me," I said, holding up my phone as I sat down beside him.

His jaw tightened, and he sighed. "What did she say?"

"Doesn't matter," I said, my voice firm. "What matters is that this can't keep happening. I need to know that you're fully in this with me, Lucas. I can't keep fighting for a relationship if I feel like I'm also fighting your past."

He didn't speak right away, staring out at the water as if searching for the right words. Finally, he turned to me, his expression serious.

"You're right," he said. "You shouldn't have to fight for this. Emily and I... were a part of each other's lives for so long, and I think a part of me felt like letting go completely would make me the bad guy. I know that holding on, even a little, is hurting you. Hurting us. And that's not fair."

I nodded, letting his words sink in. "I don't want to give you an ultimatum, Lucas. That's not who I am. But I also can't keep doing this if there's any part of you that's still tied to her."

"There isn't," he said quickly, his hand reaching for mine. "Not in the way that matters. I care about you. I want this, us. I just need to make it crystal clear to her, once and for all."

Hearing him say that should've been enough, but I knew it wasn't just about him. It was about me, too. I had to trust my instincts, my strength, and my worth.

"I care about you too," I said, squeezing his hand. "But I need to know that you'll follow through. I've worked too hard to stop being the person who avoids conflict and lets fear dictate everything. I'm not a chicken shit anymore, Lucas. I need someone strong enough to stand beside me, not someone who's caught in the past."

He nodded, his grip on my hand tightening. "You have my word. I'll handle it."

That conversation didn't magically fix everything, but it felt like a turning point, a moment where I realized just how far I'd come. I wasn't afraid to speak up, to stand my ground and demand the kind of relationship I deserved.

The chicken was no longer frozen, sizzling, or even golden. It was bold. And as I sat there on the dock with Lucas, watching the sunset paint the water in shades of orange and gold, I knew that I'd be okay.

CHAPTER SIXTEEN

Letting It Rest

Each moment I spent with Lucas felt like discovering another layer of him. His laughter, his quirks, the way he always seemed to know when I needed encouragement or just quiet. He was grounding and adventurous all at once, the kind of person who made you feel steady even when life felt like chaos. But the chaos wasn't just outside. It was creeping into the space we were trying to build, and its name was Emily.

Lucas had previously assured me that he and Emily were over and that whatever they had was in the past. But it became clear, slowly and painfully, that Emily didn't share that perspective. The calls became more frequent, the texts more urgent, and once, when we were out to dinner, she showed up.

It wasn't subtle. She walked right up to the table, her presence sharp and calculated, as if she'd rehearsed this moment a hundred times. She was beautiful in that effortless way that made me feel small, unprepared, and underdressed.

"Lucas," she said, ignoring me completely. "We need to talk."

Lucas stood, his expression a mix of frustration and concern. "Emily, not here. This isn't the time."

Her eyes flicked to me, and for a moment, I could feel her sizing me up. "I'm sure she'll understand. This is important."

I stayed quiet, my heart pounding. The old me—the chicken shit—would've shrunk into the background, let Lucas handle it, and avoided any sort of confrontation. I'd spent too much time letting other people's needs and emotions dictate my life, and I wasn't going to let it happen again.

"I do understand," I said, my voice calm but firm. "But this is neither the time nor the place for whatever it is you need to say. You'll have to wait."

She blinked, clearly not expecting me to respond, and Lucas stepped in before the situation could escalate further. "Emily, I'll call you later," he said, his tone leaving no room for argument.

She hesitated, glancing between the two of us, then turned and left without another word. The tension at the table was thick enough to cut with a knife, and as Lucas sat back down, I could feel the weight of everything unspoken between us.

"I'm sorry," he said finally, running a hand through his hair. "I didn't know she'd—"

"She's still in love with you," I interrupted, the words sharper than I intended. "I need to know if this is something you're ready to deal with. Because if you're not, I can't do this."

Lucas's eyes met mine, and I could see the conflict there. He wasn't a bad person, not by any stretch, but he was someone who struggled to let go and set boundaries when it meant hurting someone else. I cared about him, but I couldn't ignore the fact that his inability to fully close that door with Emily was hurting me.

"I care about you," he said, his voice low but steady. "I do. And I don't want to lose you. But you're right. I haven't handled this the way I should have, and that's on me. I'll talk to her. Really talk to her. Set boundaries. Because you're what I want, and I can't keep letting her interfere with that."

His words were reassuring, but I knew they weren't enough on their own. This wasn't something he could fix with promises. It was something I needed to see. And in that moment, I realized something else: whether or not Lucas followed through, whether or not this relationship worked out, I was going to be okay. I had grown. I was no longer the woman who stayed silent, who put everyone else's feelings ahead of her own, who let fear dictate her life.

The next morning, I woke up early, laced up my hiking boots, and went for a long hike in the woods near my home. It was something I'd started doing on my own, a way to clear my head and reconnect with myself. As I climbed higher, the tension in my chest started to ease, replaced by a quiet sense of clarity. The view at the top wasn't dramatic, just rolling hills and trees stretching as far as the eye could see, but it felt like freedom.

Standing there, I thought about how far I'd come. The woman I was a few months ago wouldn't have spoken up at that dinner table. She wouldn't have demanded more from Lucas or herself. She would've backed down and made herself smaller to avoid conflict.

I refused to return to the life of a chicken shit. I was strong. And no matter what happened with Lucas or Emily or anything else, I knew I'd keep moving forward, one adventure at a time because this wasn't just about him or us. This was about me. About living the life I'd spent too long avoiding.

When I got back to the car, my phone buzzed with a text from Lucas: I talked to her. It's done. I'm all in if you are.

I smiled, not because the conflict was over, but because I knew I'd be okay no matter what lay ahead. I wasn't afraid of the unknown. I was ready for it.

CHAPTER SEVENTEEN

Out of the Pan

For weeks, things with Lucas had been steady. Emily seemed to respond to the boundaries he'd set with her, and although the occasional text or voicemail still popped up, it seemed like she'd finally started to let go. I let myself believe that we'd moved past the worst of it. But as it turned out, I was wrong.

It started subtly at first, almost like background noise. A strange car parked down the street from my house, its driver obscured behind tinted windows. A bouquet left at my door without a note. My phone ringing late at night with no one on the other end. I told myself it was nothing, a coincidence, an overactive imagination, but the unease gnawed at me, growing louder with each passing day.

The reason for that unease presented itself one evening after work. I'd just pulled into my driveway when I noticed someone sitting on the porch steps. For a split second, I thought it was Lucas, but as I stepped out of the car, I realized it wasn't. It was Emily.

She looked different than the confident, calculating woman I'd met at the restaurant that night. Her hair was unkempt, her clothes wrinkled, and there was a frantic energy in her eyes that set every nerve in my body on edge.

"What are you doing here?" I asked, keeping my voice steady even though my heart was pounding.

She stood, clutching something in her hands. A framed photo. She shoved it toward me, and I recognized it instantly: a picture of Lucas and Emily, smiling and carefree, from what looked like years ago.

"You think you can just take him from me?" she snapped, her voice trembling with barely restrained anger. "You think he's yours now?"

I took a step back, my mind racing. "Emily, I don't know what you think is happening here, but Lucas made it clear—"

"Clear?" she interrupted, laughing bitterly. "You think he's yours because he said some sweet things and held your hand? You don't know him like I do. You don't understand what we had."

"I understand that it's over," I said, forcing calm into my voice. "He told you that. You need to let go."

Her expression darkened, her grip tightening on the frame. "Let go?" she repeated, her voice dropping to a dangerous whisper. "You don't get to tell me to let go. You don't get to take everything from me."

Before I could respond, she hurled the frame to the ground. The glass shattered, the sharp crack echoing in the quiet evening air. She took a step toward me, and instinctively, I backed up.

"You think you're so strong," she said, her voice laced with venom. "You're nothing. You don't deserve him."

"Emily, this isn't the way to handle this," I said, my pulse racing. I was out of my depth, but I refused to let her see how scared I was. "You need help. Please, just leave."

She laughed again, a hollow, unnerving sound, before turning and storming off down the street. I stood frozen, staring at the shattered glass on my porch until the sound of her car screeching away jolted me back to reality.

I called Lucas immediately, my hands shaking as I told him what had happened. He arrived within twenty minutes, his face pale and drawn as he listened.

"I thought she was done," he said, his voice heavy with guilt. "I thought I made it clear."

"She's not done, Lucas," I said, my voice firmer than I expected. "She's escalating. And I don't think this is something you can fix on your own."

We agreed to file a report with the police, though they could only do so much without concrete evidence of a threat. Lucas promised to stay with me for a while, at least until things settled down. But the encounter had shaken me in a way I couldn't ignore.

That night, as I lay awake with Lucas beside me, I thought about how far I'd come. The old me would've been paralyzed by fear, shrinking back into herself and letting the situation control her. But now? Now, I knew I was stronger than that. I wasn't going to let Emily—or anyone else—dictate my life.

The next morning, I signed up for a self-defense class. Not because I thought I could handle Emily on my own if she showed up again, but because I wanted to feel empowered. I wanted to know that if push came to shove, I could stand my ground.

Emily's presence loomed over us like a storm cloud, but it wouldn't break me. I wasn't the same person I'd been when this journey started. I wasn't afraid to face the storm head-on, to stand tall and protect the life I was building for myself.

I was reclaiming my power, refusing to be a victim, and proving to myself that I could rise above anything—even the chaos of someone else's obsession. The chicken wasn't just strong; it was unbreakable now. And no one, not even Emily, could take that away from me.

CHAPTER EIGHTEEN

Making the Perfect Plate

The issues with Emily reached a point I hadn't anticipated, a line I never thought she'd cross. Things between Lucas and me had finally felt stable. He'd reassured me that he was maintaining the boundaries he'd set, keeping his distance, and that she understood it was over. For weeks, everything had been quiet. Too quiet. I should have known it was the calm before the storm.

She announced her return with something small. A note left on my windshield. At first, I thought it was a flyer or maybe someone's passive-aggressive comment about my parking job. But when I unfolded it, my stomach dropped. The message was scrawled in harsh, jagged handwriting:

"You'll never mean as much to him as I do."

I stared at it, my pulse racing, half-convinced I was imagining things. But that uneasy feeling crept back in, and when I showed the note to Lucas later that evening, his jaw tightened.

"She's gone too far," he said, his voice sharp with anger. "I'll talk to her again. This has to stop."

But it didn't stop. The next day, I came home from work to find my trash cans overturned, the contents scattered across my driveway. At first, I thought it was just a raccoon or the wind, but the sight of broken glass shards from the same picture frame Emily had smashed on my porch weeks ago made my blood run cold. I knew it wasn't an accident.

I called Lucas, my voice trembling as I recounted what I'd found. He insisted on coming over, and when he arrived, he was furious. "This ends now," he said, pacing my living room. "I'll go to her place. Make her understand."

"No," I said quickly, grabbing his arm. "That's exactly what she wants. You showing up and giving her attention will just fuel whatever this is. We need to go to the police."

We did. I filed a second report, this time with photos of the note and the mess she'd made outside my house. The officer was sympathetic but cautious, explaining that without direct proof of her involvement, there wasn't much they could do. I left the station feeling more frustrated than reassured, but I refused to let that fear get to me.

That resolve was tested a few nights later.

I was home alone, curled up on the couch with a book when I heard it. A sound outside, faint but distinct. Footsteps. I froze, my heart hammering in my chest, straining to hear over the rush of blood in my ears. The steps grew louder, circling the side of the house.

Grabbing my phone, I called Lucas, my voice a shaky whisper. "Someone's outside," I said. "I think it's her."

"Stay inside. Lock the doors. I'm on my way," he said, his voice calm but urgent.

I hung up and crept to the front window, peeking out through the curtains. The street was empty, but the footsteps hadn't stopped. They were closer now, almost at the back door. I grabbed the baseball bat I kept by the door, not because I thought I could fend her off but because I needed to feel like I had something, anything, to protect myself.

Then I heard it. The doorknob rattled.

"Emily!" I shouted, my voice steady despite the panic rising inside me. "I've called the police. You need to leave now!"

The rattling stopped, replaced by silence so heavy it pressed against my ears. My pulse thundered, and for a moment, I thought she might actually be gone. But then, there was a loud bang of something hitting the back door.

Before I could react, my phone buzzed. It was Lucas. "I'm outside," he said. "Stay where you are."

Moments later, I heard his voice outside, sharp and commanding. "Emily, stop this! Now!"

I ran to the back window and saw them. Lucas was standing a few feet from Emily, who held a brick in her hand. Her face was twisted with anger, but there was something else there, too. Desperation.

"This is your fault," she spat at him, her voice shaking. "You let her take you away from me. You promised you'd always be there!"

"I never promised that, Emily," he said, his tone calm but firm. "You need help. This isn't the way to fix things."

For a moment, she hesitated, her grip on the brick loosening. Then her eyes darted to me, standing in the window, and her expression hardened.

"You don't deserve him," she said, her voice venomous.

"Emily, drop it," Lucas said, stepping closer.

The sound of sirens broke through the tension, flashing lights appearing at the end of the street. Emily's head whipped around, and she dropped the brick, her shoulders slumping as officers approached. They spoke to her briefly before placing her in handcuffs and leading her to a patrol car.

I watched the scene unfold from the safety of my house, my knees weak and my breath unsteady. When Lucas finally came inside, his face was pale but resolute.

"She's gone," he said softly, pulling me into his arms. "It's over."

I wanted to believe that, and I knew the fear wouldn't disappear overnight. Emily's actions had shaken me, but they hadn't broken me.

Lucas and I had a long road ahead, filled with conversations about boundaries, trust, and healing. But as I sat beside him that night, my hand in his, I knew one thing for certain: I had left the person that started this bucket list behind.

In fact, I wasn't that chicken shit at all anymore. I had evolved, undeterred, and I was ready for whatever came next. For the first time in a long time, I truly believed that nothing, and no one, could take that strength away from me

.

CHAPTER NINETEEN

Finishing Touches

Several weeks later, Lucas and I had spent the evening walking along the waterfront, talking about future trips we wanted to take. He was animated, describing a sailing route he'd dreamed of taking through the Caribbean, and for a brief moment, it felt like we could leave the chaos behind and move forward. It was deceptively peaceful.

But that illusion shattered when we returned to my house.

The first thing I noticed was the broken glass. My front window shattered with shards glittering on the porch like tiny daggers. My stomach sank, and a cold wave of dread washed over me. Lucas was already stepping ahead of me, his body tense, his phone in hand as he called the police.

"Stay here," he said, his voice firm but shaky.

"Lucas—" I started, but he was already inside.

Ignoring the warning bells in my head, I followed. The living room was a mess—bookshelves overturned, picture frames smashed, cushions slashed. My heart raced as I scanned the room, and that's when I saw her. Emily.

She was standing in the kitchen, holding one of my knives. Her hair was wild, her eyes red-rimmed, and there was a manic edge to her posture that made my blood run cold. Lucas froze when he saw her, raising his hands cautiously.

"Emily," he said, his voice calm but firm. "Put the knife down. This isn't you."

Her laugh was sharp and bitter. "You don't get to tell me who I am," she snapped, pointing the knife in his direction. "You don't get to walk away like none of this ever mattered."

I was rooted to the spot, my pulse thundering in my ears. Every instinct told me to run, to get out of there, but I couldn't leave Lucas.

"Emily, listen to me," I said, my voice trembling but steady enough to carry. Her eyes snapped to mine, and for a moment, I thought she might lunge.

"This is all your fault," she said, her voice cracking. "You took him from me. You ruined everything."

"You're wrong," I said, forcing myself to hold her gaze. "You're the one holding on to something that's gone. Lucas didn't ruin anything. He's just trying to move forward. And you can, too. But not like this."

Her grip on the knife tightened, and for a second, I thought she'd take a step closer. But then, the sound of sirens in the distance broke through the tension. Her face crumpled, and the knife slipped from her hand, clattering to the floor.

Lucas moved quickly, kicking the knife out of reach and stepping between Emily and me. The police arrived moments later, ushering her out of the house as she sobbed incoherently.

When they left, taking Emily with them, the house was silent except for the sound of my ragged breathing. Lucas turned to me, his face pale and drawn.

"I'm so sorry," he said, his voice heavy with guilt. "You never should've been dragged into this."

"She needed help," I said quietly, sitting down on the edge of the couch. "And now she'll get it. But Lucas... we can't keep doing this."

He looked at me, his expression pained. "What do you mean?"

I took a deep breath, gathering the strength I'd fought so hard to build. "This isn't just about Emily. It's about us. As much as I care about you, I can't ignore the toll this has taken on me. I've spent so much time trying to navigate the chaos, trying to prove that I'm strong enough to handle it, but I shouldn't have to. Love isn't supposed to feel like survival."

His shoulders slumped, and for the first time, I saw how tired he was, too. "I don't want to lose you," he said, his voice barely above a whisper.

"I don't want to lose myself," I replied.

The silence between us was heavy but honest. We both knew this wasn't a decision I'd made lightly and as much as it hurt, it felt like the right one.

Lucas stayed that night, helping me clean up the wreckage and making sure I felt safe. When he left the next morning, it was with a quiet understanding that this was goodbye.

In the weeks that followed, I focused on rebuilding—not just my home, but myself. I signed up for more adventures, leaned on the friends and family who'd supported me, and took the time to reflect on everything I'd learned.

Emily's presence had forced me to confront fears I'd buried for years, and Lucas had shown me what it felt like to connect deeply with someone. But in the end, it was my strength that carried me through.

The chicken shit version of me would've stayed, clinging to a relationship that no longer felt right out of fear of being alone. But that version no longer existed. The chicken shit was dead, and I was strong and resilient.

The end with Lucas wasn't the end of my story. It was just another step forward, another lesson learned, another reminder that I was capable of so much more than I'd ever given myself credit for. And as I stood on the threshold of a new chapter, I knew I was more than ready.

CHAPTER TWENTY

Frozen Chicken Doesn't Live Here Anymore

The flight to Bora Bora had been long, but the moment I stepped off the plane and felt the warm, salty breeze on my face, the weight of the past few months lifted. The turquoise waters stretched endlessly in every direction, the sun glinting off the gentle waves as if the ocean itself were smiling. It was stunning, the kind of beauty that pictures could never fully capture. I wasn't just seeing it. I was feeling it.

I'd booked the trip on a whim, surprising even myself. Bora Bora had been on my bucket list for years, even before the chicken shit bucket list, but it always felt like one of those "someday" things. Someday, when I had time. Someday, when I felt ready. Someday, when I wasn't too afraid to step outside of my carefully controlled w orld.

"Someday" wasn't guaranteed, so here I was, standing on the dock of a tiny overwater bungalow, my suitcase at my feet and my heart lighter than it had been in a long time.

The days passed in a blissful blur of quiet mornings sipping coffee on the deck, afternoons spent snorkeling through coral reefs, and evenings watching the sunset blaze in pink and gold. There were no deadlines, no buzzing phones, no drama. Just me, the ocean, and the kind of peace I'd spent years searching for without even realizing it.

One night, as the stars blanketed the sky, I sat on the edge of the deck, my feet dangling in the water. The lagoon was still, its surface reflecting the moonlight like a mirror. It was the kind of stillness that made you think, really think, about where you'd been and where you were go ing.

I thought about the version of me who'd started this journey, the workaholic chicken shit who'd buried herself in emails and schedules and was too scared to step outside her comfort zone. I thought about the version of me who'd stared down rapids, hiked mountain trails, soared through the sky on a zipline, and faced down the chaos of a relationship tangled in someone else's unresolved past. I thought about every adventure, every mistake, every moment I'd chosen courage over fear.

And here I was, on the other side of it all, stronger than I ever thought I could be.

I pulled out my bucket list notebook. The one I'd started months ago, now worn and dog-eared from use. Flipping through the pages, I smiled at the items I'd checked off, each one a small victory in its own right. Waterfalls in Tennessee. A hot air balloon ride. Rock climbing. Kayaking. Sailing. Each adventure had taught me something, not just about the world, but about myself.

Then, there were the lessons I hadn't planned for, the ones that came from Lucas and everything that happened with Emily. For a long time, I thought love meant holding on, fighting to keep something alive even when it wasn't working. Instead, I'd learned that sometimes, strength comes from letting go, knowing your worth, and refusing to settle for anything less than the life you deserve.

I flipped to a blank page in the notebook and wrote something new and just for me:

Sage - Keep moving forward. Always.

It wasn't a specific destination or activity, but it felt right. If this journey had taught me anything, it would have been that life isn't about reaching a finish line. It's about the moments in between, the ones where you surprise yourself, challenge yourself, and discover what it means to live.

The breeze picked up, carrying the faint scent of salt and flowers, and I leaned back, letting the stillness settle around me. Bora Bora wasn't the end of my story; it was just another chapter and another step forward.

As the stars shimmered overhead and the water lapped gently against the deck, I smiled to myself, feeling free and more alive than I ever had. I wasn't afraid of what came next. For the first time in my life, I wasn't afraid at all.

Thank You

Dear Reader,

Thank you for taking the time to read "Bucket List of a Chicken Sh*t".

I started this book in the middle of the night when I was scrolling on one of my phones. Yes, I'm a "plural phone carrier" much like Sage, and I found that her story was so easy to tell, despite the heaviness of the sleep I wasn't getting when the muse took hold.

Please, do me a favor and take a few seconds to leave a review. I would love to know what you think!

Keep moving forward, Always!

LW

Also by London Webb

Camping with Kids: How to Plan, Prepare, and Keep Your Sanity

Available on Amazon Kindle, Paperback, Hardcover, and Audible Audiobook.

Toddler Parenting: Expert Level: Tantrums Happen - How to Survive the Tornado

Available on Amazon Kindle, Paperback, Hardcover, and Audible Audiobook.

**Big Money Little People: A Parent's Guide to
Raising Financially Savvy Kids**

Available on Amazon Kindle and Paperback.

Visit My Author Page for all available titles!

www.ingramcontent.com/pod-product-compliance
Lightning Source LLC
Chambersburg PA
CBHW072035170626
46811CB00008B/3088